"Good night, good night!
parting is such sweet sorrow,
That I shall say good night
till it be morrow."

– William Shakespeare, *Romeo and Juliet*

MOPPET BOOKS

www.moppetbookspublishing.com

KinderGuides™ Early Learning Guides to Culture Classics
Published by Moppet Books
Los Angeles, California

Copyright © 2018 Moppet Books
All rights reserved including the right of reproduction in whole or in part in any form without written permission from the publisher.

ISBN: 978-0-9988205-3-8

Art direction and book design by Melissa Medina
Written by Melissa Medina and Fredrik Colting

Special thanks to:
Melody Foster, Jeannine Medina and Manny Medina

Printed in China

KinderGuides

EARLY LEARNING GUIDE TO **WILLIAM SHAKESPEARE'S**

ROMEO and JULIET

By MELISSA MEDINA *and* FREDRIK COLTING

Illustrations by MARIJKE BUURLAGE

Table *of* Contents

About the Author 6

Story Summary 8

Main Characters 40

Key Words 42

Quiz Questions 44

Analysis 46

About *the* Author

WILLIAM SHAKESPEARE

William Shakespeare was born in Stratford-upon-Avon, England, in 1564. He was a poet, playwright and actor, and is considered one of the greatest writers in the English language. In fact, he is often called England's national poet and the "Bard of Avon" (bard means poet). Shakespeare wrote a whopping 38 plays that have been translated into all major languages and are performed more often than any other plays in the world. His plays are both comedies (funny) and tragedies (super sad), and like many playwrights of his day, he wrote them sort of like long poems. His most famous plays are *Hamlet, Macbeth* and the beloved tragedy, *Romeo and Juliet,* written around 1595. Although his style of writing can be tough to understand, Shakespeare's plays are a huge part of western culture, and most students are required to read them at some point...at least twice.

In the fair Italian city of Verona, live the Montagues and the Capulets, two families that hate each other's guts.

One day, members of the two families happen to meet on the street, and they get into a terrible fight. It's so bad that the Prince has to be called in to stop the fighting.

Meanwhile, Romeo Montague, a young man who, unlike the rest of his family, is more interested in love than fighting, is pouting about a girl named Rosaline who does not return his feelings of love.

Count Paris, a wealthy relative of the Prince, is also looking for love, or at least a wife. He's heard that Juliet Capulet is the most beautiful girl in Verona, so he asks her father for her hand in marriage. Lord Capulet happily agrees, but says that Juliet is still too young to marry. He asks Paris to wait two years, but says that he can spend time with Juliet at a masquerade party that evening at the Capulet house.

Lord Capulet makes a list of people to invite to the party and gives it to his servant. The servant has a problem though—he can't read. So when he comes across Romeo and Romeo's cousin, Benvolio, on the street, he asks them to read the names for him. Romeo spots Rosaline's name on the list, so they decide to sneak into the Capulet party that night.

In the Capulet house, servants are busy preparing for the masquerade. Lady Capulet calls for her daughter, Juliet, and tells her that she should start thinking about marriage. She's heard that Count Paris is interested in Juliet, and he would be a great catch. Juliet is not super excited, but agrees to meet Paris at the party to see if she could possibly like him.

The party is in full swing when Romeo, Benvolio, and Romeo's best friend, Mercutio, sneak in, wearing masks. Romeo looks for Rosaline but instead he spots Juliet from across the room. She's the most beautiful girl he has ever seen! He tries to get closer to her when Tybalt, Juliet's cousin, recognizes Romeo as a Montague. Immediately he wants to fight Romeo, but Lord Capulet says there will be no fighting at his party!

Romeo approaches Juliet and touches her hand. They begin to talk and, just like that, they fall madly in love.

However, after the party, they are both told that they belong to enemy families and can never meet again. They are both devastated.

Despite the danger of getting caught, Romeo decides to see Juliet again and climbs the wall to enter the Capulet orchard. Benvolio and Mercutio call out for him, but Romeo pretends he can't hear them, and they leave.

Juliet soon appears on the balcony above where Romeo is hiding. She talks to herself and wonders why Romeo must be a Montague, when their two families are enemies. Suddenly Romeo steps out from the shadows, surprising her. They confess their love for each other and, just like that, agree to marry. Juliet then tells Romeo that he must leave because if her family finds him there, they will surely kill him. She promises to send a messenger for him the next day, and Romeo bids her farewell.

Early the next day, Romeo visits his friend, Friar Laurence, to tell him that he intends to marry Juliet. The Friar is surprised to hear that Romeo has so quickly forgotten about Rosaline, but nevertheless agrees to marry them, as he thinks it might end the fighting between their families.

Later that morning, Romeo meets up with Benvolio and Mercutio and they find out that Juliet's cousin, Tybalt, has challenged Romeo to a duel. This is worrying because Tybalt is known as a master swordsman, and Romeo does not want to fight any of his dear Juliet's relatives. For now though, all he can think about is marrying her. When he sees Juliet's nurse approach, he gives her a message for Juliet to meet him at Friar Laurence's that afternoon so they can be married.

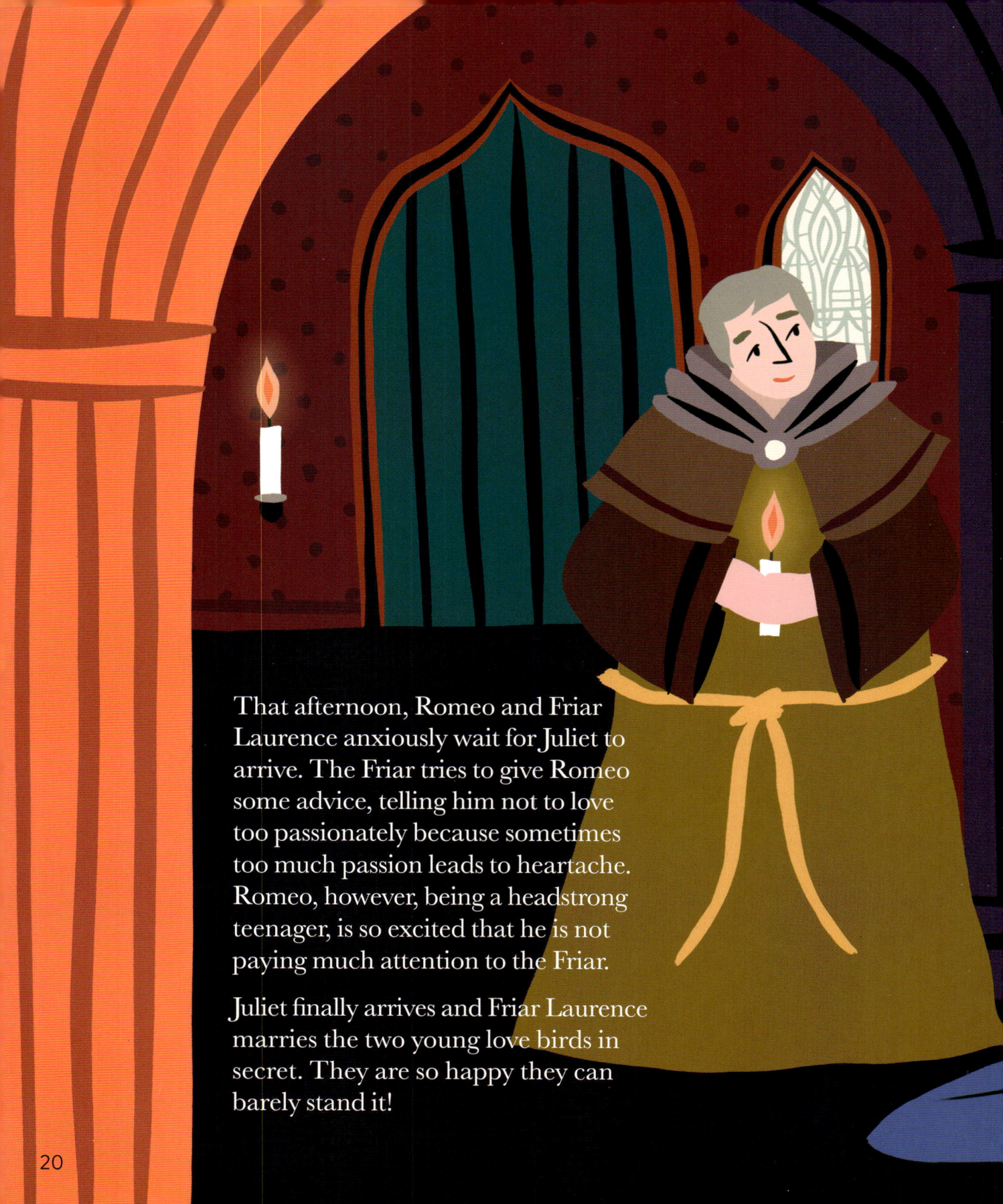

That afternoon, Romeo and Friar Laurence anxiously wait for Juliet to arrive. The Friar tries to give Romeo some advice, telling him not to love too passionately because sometimes too much passion leads to heartache. Romeo, however, being a headstrong teenager, is so excited that he is not paying much attention to the Friar.

Juliet finally arrives and Friar Laurence marries the two young love birds in secret. They are so happy they can barely stand it!

Knowing their families will never accept it, Romeo and Juliet decide to keep their marriage a secret, and they each return home after the wedding.

On his way home, Romeo meets Benvolio and Mercutio in the street where they are being taunted by Tybalt and his men. Tybalt is still mad about Romeo crashing the Capulet party, and draws his sword, challenging Romeo to fight. But Romeo refuses.

Instead, Mercutio, who is very quick-witted, taunts Tybalt into fighting him instead. Romeo tries to stop them, but in the scuffle Tybalt's sword goes right through Mercutio, who dies.

Romeo, enraged by the death of his dear friend, reacts in blind anger. He draws his sword and kills Tybalt, then quickly runs away. When the Prince arrives at the scene he is so angry at Romeo that he banishes him from Verona forever.

The Nurse rushes into Juliet's room with news of the fight and Tybalt's death. Juliet is devastated, but she knows that Romeo is not to blame. She gives the Nurse her ring to give to Romeo so he will know that she forgives him and wants him by her side.

Romeo, not knowing where to turn, is hiding at the monastery with Friar Laurence. The Friar tells him that he is lucky that the Prince has decided not to kill him, but only banish him from the city. Romeo, however, is more concerned about Juliet. What will she think of him now? The Nurse arrives and gives Romeo Juliet's ring as a symbol of her love, which makes him feel better. Together with the Friar they come up with a plan where Romeo will spend the wedding night with Juliet, then flee to a nearby town called Mantua, to wait for her to join him.

The Nurse sneaks Romeo into Juliet's room that night, and they are so happy to be together again. The next morning, they tearfully part, knowing Romeo must leave, or the Capulets will capture him. Before he goes, Romeo promises Juliet that they will see each other again.

Just after Romeo leaves, Juliet's parents come in and tell her that she is to marry Count Paris that very week instead of waiting two years. They have no idea that she is already married to Romeo. Juliet refuses, and her father becomes furious and says he will disown her if she does not marry Paris!

Juliet feels like the only person she can trust is Friar Laurence, so she goes to seek his advice. She tells him that she would rather die than marry Paris! The Friar wants to help her and suggests a plan. Juliet will pretend to agree to marry Paris, and on the night before the wedding she will drink a sleeping potion that will make her appear dead for two days. Her family will then put her in a tomb and the Friar will send for Romeo to come get her. Then they can live happily ever after! Juliet agrees to the plan and leaves with the sleeping potion.

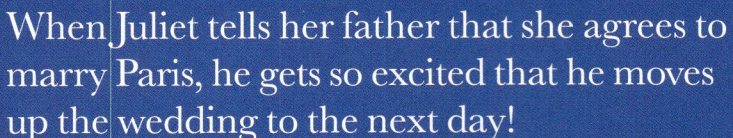

When Juliet tells her father that she agrees to marry Paris, he gets so excited that he moves up the wedding to the next day!

That night, Juliet tells her nurse that she wants to be alone. She holds the sleeping potion and wonders what will happen when she drinks it. What if she really dies? She is scared, but then she thinks of Romeo and empties the bottle into her mouth.

The next morning, as the Nurse comes into the room to wake her, she finds Juliet lying lifeless in her bed. The entire house is in uproar over Juliet's death. Soon Friar Laurence arrives and says that they must prepare for Juliet's funeral instead of her wedding.

When Romeo hears the news that Juliet is dead his heart fills with sorrow. He decides that he will go to Juliet's tomb to see her one last time. But before he leaves, he buys a vial of poison to drink at the tomb. He does not want to live without Juliet!

Meanwhile, Friar Laurence learns that the letter he sent to Romeo explaining the plan was never delivered. Oh no! He realizes that he will have to go get Juliet out of the tomb himself, and then Romeo can meet her at the monastery.

He doesn't know that Romeo has already been told about Juliet's death and is on his way to her.

At the cemetery, Count Paris arrives and begins scattering flowers near Juliet's tomb. After all, he is really sad too. Suddenly he hears Romeo approaching. Wanting to avenge the deaths of Tybalt and Juliet, Paris lunges to attack Romeo. Romeo pleads with Paris to leave him alone, but Paris will not listen. As Romeo tries to defend himself, Paris is the one who gets killed.

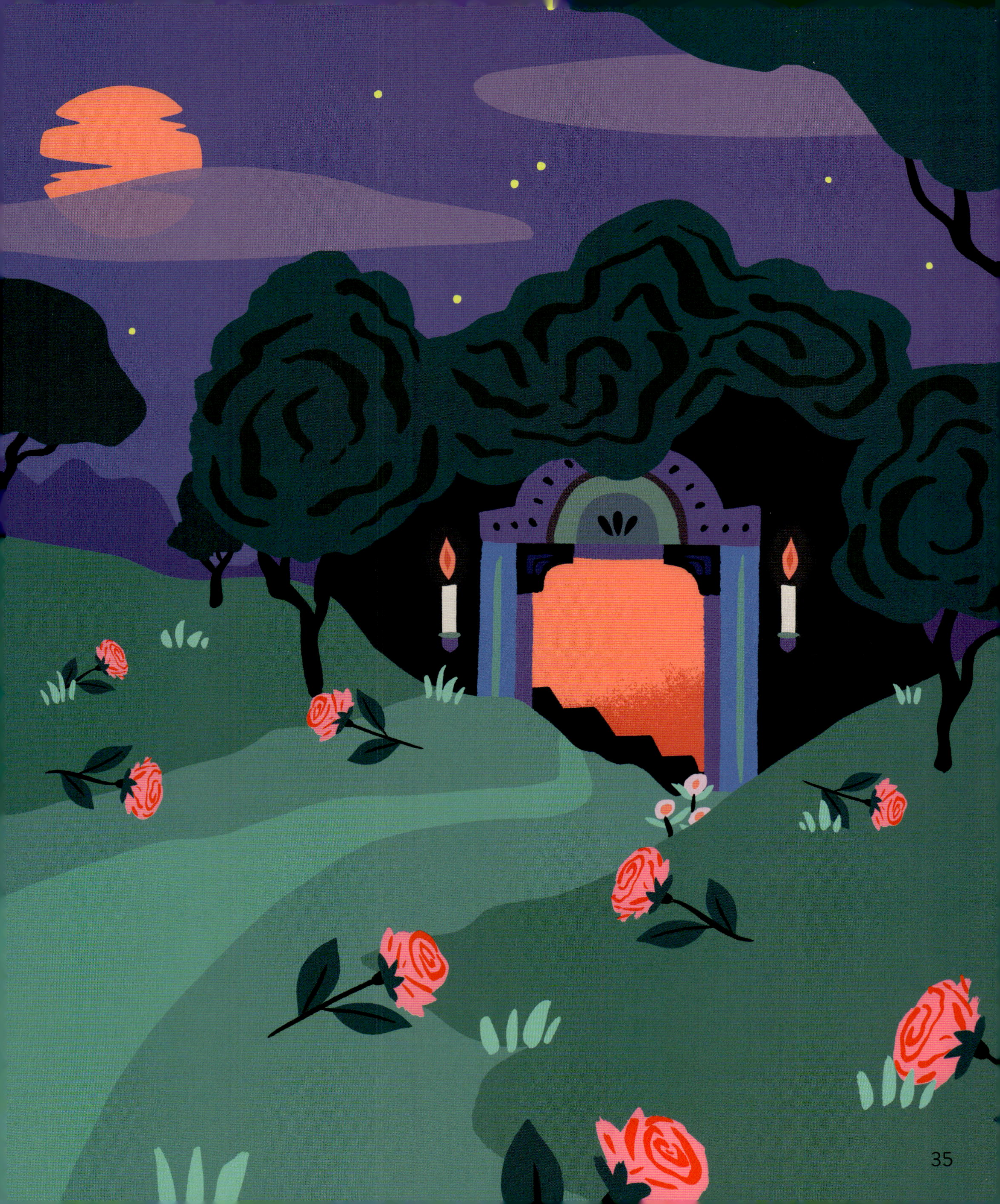

Romeo enters the tomb and finds Juliet. She looks more beautiful than ever, as if she's not really dead at all. Seeing her there, Romeo only wants one thing: to spend the rest of eternity with his lovely wife. So with tears in his eyes, he drinks the vial of poison, kisses Juliet on the lips, and dies.

As Friar Laurence enters the tomb, Juliet suddenly wakes from her deep sleep. She immediately asks for Romeo. Friar Laurence tells her that both Romeo and Paris are dead. At the same time, voices are heard from outside the tomb, and the Friar tells Juliet that they must hurry to get out. But she refuses to leave her husband's side.

As the Friar leaves, a heartbroken Juliet takes Romeo's knife and pushes it into her chest, then falls over his body and dies.

Soon the Prince arrives with Juliet's father. Then Romeo's father arrives as well. Friar Laurence finally tells them the story of Romeo and Juliet's secret marriage. The Prince scolds Lords Capulet and Montague and tells them that it was their hatred for each other that caused this tragedy.

The two fathers realize how awful they've been. And although it's too late to save Romeo and Juliet, they agree to build a golden statue to honor the young couple's love for each other, and to finally end the family feud and live in peace.

Main Characters

Romeo

is a member of the Montague family and he's the most passionate and emotional young man you can imagine. Love is the only thing that matters to him, but sometimes he doesn't quite think things through. Although he is a good person, his untamed passion proves to be a problem.

Juliet

is the beautiful teenage daughter of the Capulet family who turns heads wherever she goes. Although younger than Romeo, she is more level-headed than he is and is guided by her strong principles as well as her intense love and loyalty to him.

Lord & Lady Capulet
are Juliet's parents and the Montague's enemies. Although they love their daughter very much, they try to control her.

Nurse
is Juliet's caretaker and has been since she was a baby. She would do anything for Juliet.

Tybalt
is Juliet's cousin and a bit of a hot-head. He gets into a fight with Mercutio, and kills him.

Friar Laurence
is the only person Romeo and Juliet can confide in. He marries them and later tries to help them escape.

Benvolio
is Romeo's thoughtful and level-headed cousin. He is always trying to cheer Romeo up.

Lord & Lady Montague
are Romeo's parents. They love their son deeply, but are always fighting with the Capulets.

Count Paris
is a handsome, arrogant, and wealthy relative of the Prince, who is also Lord Capulet's chosen suitor to marry Juliet.

Mercutio
is Romeo's best friend. He is extremely clever, quick-witted, and quick-tempered.

Key Words

VERONA
The city in northern Italy where Romeo and Juliet live. Perhaps this story is why it's called "the city of love."

FAMILY FEUD
The Montague and the Capulet families have long been bitter enemies, and they can't seem to stop fighting–even though they probably can't remember what they are fighting about.

TEENAGERS
We all know what teenagers are, but what does it FEEL like to be a teenager? Well, just like Romeo and Juliet, teenagers usually feel intense emotions, like their hearts might suddenly just burst open.

REBELLION
When you no longer want to follow the rules you might rebel or start a rebellion; like Romeo and Juliet marrying even though their parents don't approve.

PASSION

This is a feeling that is so strong it overpowers all other feelings, and sometimes passion leads to people making choices they haven't really thought through.

FATE

This is when things happen that you have no control over. Some people believe that it was just meant to happen that way.

DUEL

In the old days when people had an argument they sometimes settled it with a sword fight, called a duel. Tybalt challenges Romeo to a duel for crashing the Capulet party.

POISON

This is something that you eat or drink that makes you so sick it might even kill you. In the end, Romeo drinks poison because he can't stand the idea of living without Juliet.

Quiz Questions

1 **Where do Romeo and Juliet live?**
A. Barcelona, Spain
B. Verona, Italy
C. London, England

2 **Who does Juliet's father want her to marry?**
A. Romeo
B. Tybalt
C. Count Paris

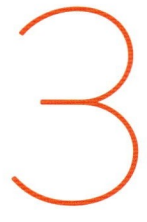

3 **Where does Romeo first see Juliet?**
A. Under a Sycamore tree
B. At a masquerade party
C. On her balcony

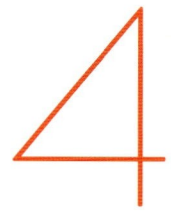

4 **Who helps Romeo and Juliet throughout the story?**
A. Juliet's mother
B. Romeo's cousin, Benvolio
C. Friar Laurence

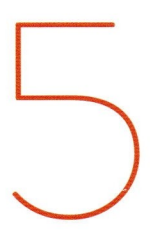

5 **Why does Romeo have to hide?**
  A. He doesn't want to be bothered by Juliet's nurse
  B. The Prince banishes him for killing Tybalt
  C. He is trying to get out of doing his chores

6 **What does Friar Laurence give Juliet?**
  A. A vial of sleeping potion
  B. A gold ring
  C. A basket of flowers

7 **What happens to Romeo and Juliet?**
  A. They have a fight and break up
  B. They move to Mantua to get away from it all
  C. They die in the tomb

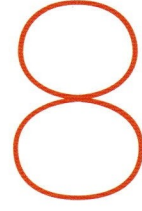

8 **What do the fathers do at the end of the story?**
  A. They build a gold statue to honor Romeo and Juliet
  B. They agree to end their family feud
  C. All of the above

ANSWER KEY: 1:B / 2:C / 3:B / 4:C / 5:C / 6:A / 7:C / 8:C

Analysis

Romeo and Juliet is a very old story about two teenagers who fall madly and deeply in love. It is **the most famous, and tragic, love story in the world.** A story is "tragic" when it is full of one sad disaster after another—as if it was doomed from the start. In fact, Shakespeare even tells us at the beginning of this story that it will NOT end well. But why would a love story be tragic, you might ask? Shakespeare shows us how sometimes **the adult world is complicated,** and even a pure love requires more than just passion.

First of all, Romeo's and Juliet's families are bitter enemies over things that have happened in the past. They probably can't even remember what they are fighting about, but both sides are too prideful to call it off. Secondly, Juliet's father just wants her to marry Count Paris because he is rich and powerful. When Romeo and Juliet fall in love, however, everything is turned upside down. They don't see each other as enemies, and don't care which families they are from. Their intense love and passion make them blind to everything else.

So while one part of Shakespeare's story is about an innocent and youthful love between Romeo and Juliet, the other part is about the opposite emotion: hate. Feeling angry and hateful and wanting to get back at someone for something they've done, is also a natural feeling, but once you give in to anger, things quickly go badly. For example, most of the terrible events in *Romeo and Juliet* happen because of anger and revenge. Tybalt kills Mercutio because Romeo snuck into the Capulet's party, and then Romeo kills Tybalt to avenge Mercutio. Romeo is so angry that he does not stop to think about what his attack on Tybalt will mean for him and Juliet. Just how love makes Romeo and Juliet blind, anger and hate can also make people blind.

With this tragic ending, Shakespeare shows us how sometimes too much passion can lead us to do things we haven't thought through, and **anger and revenge always do more harm than good.**